To Doris Freedman Schofield

Skates!

by Ezra Jack Keats

FOUR WINDS PRESS   NEW YORK

Skates!

Oooooph!

Mama!

Papa!

Oh!

Aaagh!

I've had it!

Yeah! Who wants
to skate anyway?

Library of Congress Cataloging in Publication Data

Keats, Ezra Jack.
    Skates:

    SUMMARY: Two dogs almost give up their efforts to learn to
roller skate until they have an opportunity to help a stranded kit-
ten.
    [1. Roller skating—Fiction. 2. Dogs—Fiction. 3. Stories without
words] I. Title.
PZ7.K2253Sk 1981   [E]   80-70119
ISBN 0-590-07812-7

Published by Four Winds Press
A division of Scholastic Inc., New York, N.Y.
Copyright © 1973 by Ezra Jack Keats
All rights reserved
Printed in the United States of America
Library of Congress Catalog Card Number: 80-70119
1 2 3 4 5 85 84 83 82 81